CASE FILES OF DETECTIVE SARAH JENSEN

I am dedicating this book to my Mother Virginia Brewer and Grandmother Pearl Thomas Enjoy your rest in heaven and keep those Angels looking down on me as I make this story telling be a success in my life... I love yall and one day I will see you all soon.

Epilogue

The highway stretched behind her like a forgotten memory, a path she had traveled countless times in search of justice. Sarah Jensen stood on the edge of a quiet meadow, the cool breeze rustling the tall grass around her. The sun dipped below the horizon, casting a golden glow over the tranquil scene—a stark contrast to the horrors she had unraveled.

The hunt for the C.K. Killer had tested her in ways she never imagined. The small town, with its picturesque facade, had concealed unspeakable secrets. Hidden within its shadows was the truth she had spent years chasing, a labyrinth of lies, fear, and unimaginable cruelty.

Sarah had found him—not in the way she expected, not as a faceless monster lurking in the dark, but as a man hiding in plain sight. The evidence had been buried deep, but her relentless determination and the courage of those who dared to speak had brought it to light. The killer's arrest had been swift, and the community, once complicit in silence, now faced the weight of their shared guilt.

For Sarah, victory was bittersweet. The faces of the victims still haunted her, their stolen lives a grim reminder of the price of failure. Yet, in their names, she had reclaimed a measure of peace, offering closure to their grieving families and perhaps, to herself.

As the first stars appeared in the evening sky, Sarah closed her eyes and took a deep breath. She had given everything to this case—her time, her heart, her sanity—and now it was over. The highway would always be a scar on the landscape of her life, but it no longer held the power to control her.

For the first time in years, Sarah Jensen felt the faint stirrings of hope. She had faced the darkness, and though it had left its mark, she had emerged on the other side. The road ahead was hers to choose, no longer dictated by the shadow of the C.K. Killer.

And for the first time, she was ready to move forward.

Chapter 1: The Death of Diana

10 years ago when she first got this case, the biting chill of the March wind whipped through Rogersville, Pennsylvania, a small town nestled a midst the rolling hills of the Appalachian Mountains. Detective Sarah Jensen, her face etched with determination, stepped out of her car, her eyes scanning the desolate stretch of Highway 27 that bisected the town. its dark ribbon disappearing into the horizon like a promise of endless pursuit. For the past 10 years, since the lost of her childhood friend and foster sister.. This road had been her companion, a silent witness to her relentless pursuit of a phantom, a specter that haunted the highways of America – The C.K Killer.

His victims were young, beautiful women, their lives snuffed out with brutal assault, their bodies found along the roadside, discarded like forgotten trash. Sarah had seen the terror in their lifeless eyes, the frozen screams etched on their faces. They were more than just cases to her; they were the embodiment of her own personal tragedy, a haunting reminder of the young woman who had set her life on this path.

Diana Hollis, her best friend and foster sister, had been the first victim. A bright, vivacious girl, she had fallen prey to the allure of the drug life, her innocence shattered by the harsh realities of addiction. Sarah had tried to pull her back, to guide her out of the darkness, but her efforts had proven futile. One fateful night, Diana's body had been found along the highway, her life extinguished by a brutal hand.

Sarah's heart had shattered with Diana's death, but from the ashes of her grief, a burning determination had ignited. She vowed to bring the killer to justice, to honor Diana's memory by ensuring that no other young woman would suffer the same fate.

Over the years, Sarah had become a relentless hunter, her life consumed by the pursuit of The C.K Killer. She had followed his trail across the country, piecing together fragments of evidence, tracking his movements like a bloodhound on the scent of prey.

Her obsession had not gone unnoticed. Her superiors had warned her, pleaded with her to relinquish the case, to seek solace in a life beyond the pursuit of shadows. But Sarah refused to be deterred. She was driven by an unwavering belief that justice would prevail, that the darkness could not forever eclipse the light.

For years, this highway had been a silent witness to the town's dark underbelly, a place where shadows lingered and secrets festered. It was here, on this very road, that Sarah had received her first murder case, a case that would forever change the course of her life.

Sarah, a seasoned detective with a reputation for her tenacity and loyalty, this case was never assigned to her but she took on this case to make sure that the killer will be brought to justice and pay for what he did to her foster sister and best friend.. She knew that this was no ordinary murder, that the killer had crossed a line, leaving a trail of fear and uncertainty in their wake.

As she began her investigation, Sarah knew that about the history of Diana had been struggling with addiction, since she was first awarded to the state of Pennsylvania at 12 years old. She tried everything to keep Diana from heading to a downward spiral of drugs and despair. She had been a lost soul, adrift in a sea of her own making.

The more Sarah knew about Diana, the more she felt a deep connection to the victim and her child hood friend. Diana was more than just a case; she was a reflection of Sarah's own past, a reminder of the path she had almost taken.

Sarah's determination to bring Diana's killer to justice intensified, fueled by a sense of personal responsibility. She vowed to honor Diana's memory by ensuring that no other young woman would suffer the same fate.

Over the last ten years during her investigation, this led Sarah down a dark and winding path, through the underbelly of Rogersville, where secrets were buried deep and loyalty ran thin. She faced resistance from those who wanted the case to remain unsolved, those who preferred the shadows to the harsh light of truth.

But Sarah was undeterred, her resolve unwavering. She followed the trail of evidence, no matter how faint, her determination burning brighter with each passing day.

Along the way, she encountered a cast of suspects, each with their own secrets and motivations. There was John Doe, a loner with a dark past, his eyes holding a depth of darkness that sent chills down Sarah's spine. There was Officer Mullins, a seasoned cop with a hidden agenda, his motives shrouded in mystery. And then there was Diana's best friend, a young woman grappling with her own demons, her memories of Diana haunted by guilt and regret.

As Sarah inched closer to the truth, she found herself entangled in a web of deceit and danger. The killer, lurking in the shadows, was watching her every move, waiting for the moment to strike again.

But Sarah was not afraid. She had faced darkness before, and she knew that she could face it again. She was determined to bring Diana's killer to justice, to honor her memory and bring peace to the troubled town of Rogersville.

On June 10th at 2:34am a call from a possible witness gave hope and momental to the investigation. A older truck driver had witnessed a suspicious incident on the highway, few days before the latest victim of Tammy Williams, who was a very beautiful black woman in her late teen years around 19 years old who half dressed body was found alone side of a highway in Binghamton, New York. The trucker seen a Red Peterbilt truck pulling over to the side of the road and then dragging what looks like a body out of the back. The truck driver had managed to get a partial license plate number, a lead that Sarah had been desperately seeking for months.

Hope surged through her veins, a renewed sense of purpose fueling Detective Sarah Jensen's determination. She tracked the rusted red Semi truck to a small town about 75 miles east of Rogersville, a sleepy rest area nestled a midst the quiet town of Fairview, Ohio, along Interstate seventy west. The sounds of idle semi-truck engines filled the air with the smell of diesel fumes as Sarah approached the scene, her heart pounding with anticipation.

There, she found John Doe, a young white man who looks to be around 37 years old a seemingly unassuming loner with no criminal record. Yet, a gut feeling, an intuition that ran deep within her bones, told Sarah that she had finally come face to face with the elusive C.K Killer. As she and her fellow officer approached John Doe, questioning him about his recent whereabouts 3 days ago, tension hung in the air like a thick fog.

John Doe, his demeanor calm and collected, claimed innocence. He spoke of heading west to visit family in Chicago, Illinois, a journey originating from his home in Pittsburgh, Pennsylvania. As he explained, he pulled out a meticulously kept log book and fuel receipt from the last gas station he had stopped at, a station over 200 miles from where the latest victim, Diana and Tammy, had met their tragic end.

"This can't be him," Officer Mullins interjected, skeptical of the evidence stacking against John Doe. "He has an alibi, a receipt, his log book, and he's miles away from the crime scene. Plus, we can't just rely on the passing truck driver's account. It might be a mistake with a partial tag number."

But Sarah's instincts remain to be very sure. She couldn't shake the feeling that John Doe was the key to unraveling the mystery that had plagued the nation for years. As she scrutinized the evidence before her, doubt gnawed at the edges of her conviction.

Despite the seemingly airtight alibi, Sarah pressed on. She delved into the details, cross-referencing timelines and reexamining the passing truck driver's statement. Every fiber of her being urged her to trust her intuition, to look beyond the surface of John Doe's alibi.

In the small town of Fairview, surrounded by the hum of semi-truck engines and the stillness of the night, the line between justice and doubt blurred. The pursuit of truth hung in the balance as Sarah Jensen grappled with the possibility that The C.K KILLER might slip through her fingers once again.

Chapter 2: Shadows of Doubt

The small town of Fairview lay silent beneath the vast canvas of the night sky. Detective Sarah Jensen stood at the crossroads of certainty and doubt, her mind wrestling with the conflicting narratives before her. The hum of semi-truck engines became a symphony of uncertainty as she grappled with the seemingly airtight alibi that shielded John Doe from her suspicions.

As Sarah stared at the receipt in John Doe's hands, her gaze shifted between the document and the map spread out on the hood of her squad car. The receipt detailed a transaction at a gas station far removed from the haunting scene of Diana's demise. Every logical fiber in her being urged her to accept the evidence, to acknowledge that perhaps her pursuit had led her astray.

Yet, her instincts, that primal voice echoing from the depths of her experience, whispered a different truth. The CK KILLER was elusive, cunning, and always one step ahead. Sarah had learned to trust the silent cues, the unspoken language of a seasoned detective's intuition. The shadows of doubt clung to her, threatening to overshadow the clarity she sought.

Officer Mullin observed Sarah closely, sensing the internal struggle etched across her features. "Sarah, this guy's got an alibi. We can't ignore the facts," he cautioned, his voice a counterpoint to the turmoil brewing within her.

Sarah sighed, her breath a visible manifestation of the conflict raging within. "I know, Mike. It's just... something doesn't add up. The timing, the pattern. It's too perfect and look rehearsed. I can't shake the feeling that we're being played."

As she spoke, Sarah's gaze fixated on the map, tracing the intricate web of highways and crime scenes that had eluded her for years. The killer's calculated moves formed a chilling dance, leaving her perpetually in the shadows, forever chasing a suspect.

Her mind became a battlefield of reason and instinct. The alibi held the promise of closure, a chance to end the nightmare that had haunted the nation. Yet, the nagging sensation persisted—an itch she couldn't ignore.

In the quiet of Fairview, the stars bore witness to Sarah's internal struggle. The town, bathed in moonlight, seemed to hold its breath, waiting for the detective to make a choice that would either unveil the true face of The CK KILLER or lead her down a path of deception.

Sarah's decision weighed heavily on her shoulders as she locked eyes with John Doe, the man with the airtight alibi. The chase had become a labyrinth of uncertainty, and as she stepped into the shadows, she knew that every move could either illuminate the truth or plunge her deeper into the enigmatic abyss of the C.K KILLER mind.

The Web Tightens

The haunting melody of uncertainty echoed through the dimly lit corridors of Sarah Jensen's mind, a relentless symphony of doubts and unresolved questions. The airtight alibi of John Doe AKA Mr. Greg Abbott Jr. stood like an impenetrable fortress, shielding him from the weight of suspicion. Yet, Sarah's instincts, honed over years of chasing elusive shadows, whispered a different truth.

The town of Rogersville, once a haven of tranquility, now seemed to hold its breath, its silence a deafening echo of Sarah's inner turmoil. The shadows seemed to lengthen, their tendrils reaching out to ensnare her in a labyrinth of doubt.

Sarah's gaze fell upon the map spread across her desk, a tangle of highways and crime scenes, each location a grim reminder of the C.K KILLER chilling reign of terror. The killer, a phantom lurking in the shadows, had always been one step ahead, leaving a trail of shattered lives in his wake.

A sense of frustration gnawed at Sarah's resolve. The elusive mastermind had always managed to slip through her grasp, his identity shrouded in an impenetrable veil of secrecy. The seemingly airtight alibi of Mr. Greg Abbott Jr. only served to amplify her frustration, threatening to extinguish the flame of hope that had fueled her relentless pursuit.

She meticulously scrutinized the receipt and his log book, the seemingly innocuous piece of paper that held the key to Mr. Greg Abbott Jr alibi. The date, the time, the location – every detail aligned with his story, creating an impenetrable barrier of credibility.

Yet, Sarah's instincts refused to be silenced. A nagging sense of unease persisted, a whisper from the depths of her experience that urged her to question the seemingly obvious. The timing, the pattern, the meticulousness of the alibi – it all felt too perfect, too calculated.

As the shadows deepened, Sarah found herself drawn into a labyrinth of her own making, a maze of doubt and uncertainty. The lines between truth and deception blurred, leaving her questioning her own perceptions and casting a shadow of doubt over her relentless pursuit.

The specter of The C.K KILLER loomed large, his elusiveness casting a pall of fear and anticipation over the narrative. Sarah Jensen, constantly questioning the validity of Mr. Greg Abbott Jr alibi and wondering if Sarah's instincts will prove correct or if the killer will once again slip through her grasp.

On the Trail of Shadows

Two weeks had passed since Detective Sarah Jensen's encounter with Mr. Greg Abbott Jr., the man with the seemingly airtight alibi. The shadow of doubt lingered, gnawing at her resolve, but her determination remained unwavering. She couldn't shake the nagging feeling that something was amiss, that the truth lay hidden beneath the veneer of Mr. Greg Abbott Jr.'s carefully constructed narrative.

Sarah's pursuit had taken her beyond the confines of her jurisdiction, into the head of Mr. Greg Abbott Jr.'s life. She delved into his past, scrutinizing his records, seeking any hint of deception or a connection to the C.K KILLER trail.

The more she investigated, the more intrigued she became. Mr. Greg Abbott Jr.'s life was a paradox, a puzzle of contradictions. His background was unremarkable, his financial records impeccable, his social interactions limited. Yet, there was an underlying enigma, a sense of mystery that shrouded his existence.

As Sarah delved deeper, she received the cell phone records from a warrant that she had issued to the phone company provider.. Mr. Greg Abbott Jr. phone records showed a series of cryptic calls, calls made to locations that coincided with the C.K KILLER crimes. The timing was uncanny, the pattern too precise to be mere coincidence.

The discovery sent a surge of adrenaline through Sarah's veins. The alibi, once a formidable barrier, now seemed to crumble under the weight of this new evidence. The seemingly innocent receipt and his log book, the meticulously crafted alibi, now appeared to be a carefully constructed fake, a mask hiding the true nature of the man behind the name Mr. Greg Abbott Jr..

With renewed determination, Sarah delved into the details of the cryptic calls, tracing them back to abandoned payphones, their locations scattered across the country. Each call served as a chilling reminder of the C.K KILLER presence, a haunting echo of his deadly path.

The puzzle was beginning to take shape, the pieces slowly aligning to reveal a sinister truth. Mr. Greg Abbott Jr.'s alibi was a clever deception, a smokescreen designed to divert suspicion from his true identity. The cryptic calls, the meticulous alibis, the calculated movements – they all pointed to one inescapable conclusion: Mr. Greg Abbott Jr. was The C.K KILLER.

Sarah's heart pounded with a mixture of anticipation and dread. She had been chasing this phantom for years, and now, finally, the truth lay within her grasp. The weight of responsibility pressed upon her shoulders, the knowledge that she held the key to bringing justice to the victims and their families and her child hood best friend.... Diana Hollis.

With a renewed sense of urgency, Sarah set out to unravel the remaining threads of the puzzle. She tracked down the locations of the abandoned payphones, each site a potential clue to the killer's whereabouts. The trail led her through desolate highways, forgotten towns, and abandoned buildings, each step bringing her closer to her quarry.

The chase was on, a relentless pursuit through the labyrinthine depths of Mr. Greg Abbott Jr.'s twisted mind. Sarah knew she was facing a dangerous adversary, a man driven by a dark and insatiable hunger. But her determination was unwavering, fueled by the memory of Diana and the countless victims who had fallen prey to the C.K KILLER insatiable blood lust.

The shadows that had haunted Sarah for years were beginning to recede, replaced by a glimmer of hope, a flickering light in the darkness. The truth lay just within her grasp, and Sarah was determined to bring it to light, to finally bring an end to the C.K KILLER reign of terror.

CHAPTER 3: Vanishing Act

It was a late Saturday night, just a few days before the Fourth of July. Sarah Jensen was working late in her office, poring over the maps and roads that marked the 14 murder scenes associated with the elusive C.K. Killer. The fluorescent lights overhead cast harsh shadows on her face, reflecting the grim determination etched in her eyes.

As she studied the maps, her mind raced, piecing together fragments of evidence, searching for patterns, for anything that could lead her to the killer. The case had consumed her life for years, and the weight of it pressed heavily upon her shoulders.

Suddenly, the door to the evidence room swung open, and Officer Mike Mullins stepped in. He was startled to see Sarah there, her face illuminated by the glow of the computer screen, a Coors Light beer in her hand, and a look of intense concentration etched on her features.

"Sarah?" Mike exclaimed, his voice laced with surprise. "What are you doing here?"

Sarah turned around, startled by the intrusion, but her expression quickly regained its composure. "I couldn't sleep," she replied simply, gesturing to the maps and photos that covered the walls. "I keep thinking about this case, about the victims, about the killer who's still out there."

Mike nodded understandingly. He knew how deeply this case affected Sarah. He had seen the toll it had taken on her, the way it had consumed her thoughts and dreams.

"I get it," he said, taking a seat opposite her. "I can't shake it either. It's like this killer is always one step ahead of us, always taunting us... well he is taunting you."

Sarah sighed, taking a sip of her beer. "I know," she agreed, her voice heavy with frustration. "We've been chasing this guy for years, and we still haven't gotten anywhere. It's like we're chasing a ghost."

Mike leaned forward, his eyes scanning the maps intently. "But we can't give up, Sarah. We have to keep trying. We owe it to the victims, to their families."

Sarah nodded, a flicker of determination rekindling in her eyes. "You're right, Mike. We can't give up. Not now."

They fell into a comfortable silence, each lost in their own thoughts, their minds consumed by the haunting case that had brought them together. The shadows danced around them, playing tricks on their minds, but they remained focused, their resolve unwavering.

As the night wore on, Sarah and Mike continued to sift through the evidence, searching for any clue, any hint that could lead them to The C.K KILLER. They knew that the road ahead would be long and arduous, but they were determined to see it through.

The chase was on, and the stakes were higher than ever. Sarah and Mike were united in their pursuit of justice, their determination fueled by the memory of the victims and the unwavering belief that they would ultimately prevail.

Sarah asked mike why was he there at 2am in the morning, mike replied that he think that he left something in the evidence locker. Sarah brushed the idea that mike was not telling the truth because she was too busy thinking about her evidence. Sarah was gazed and jumped up and said, lets listen to the phone call from the old truck driver who witness the dumping of Tammy Williams body in Binghamton, New York

So Sarah and Mike pulled out the recording to the interview of Rafael Fernando The old truck driver's voice echoed through the dimly lit evidence room, his words painting a chilling picture of the night he witnessed the dumping of Tammy Williams' body in Binghamton, New York. Sarah Jensen and Officer Mike Mullins listened intently, their faces etched with concentration as they absorbed every detail of the account.

The old truck driver's voice was gravelly, his words laced with a hint of fear and uncertainty and a slight broken English. He spoke of a large truck, its headlights cutting through the darkness, and a figure emerging from the shadows, dragging a lifeless body towards the roadside.

Sarah's mind raced, connecting the dots, piecing together fragments of evidence from the past murders. The truck driver's account aligned with the pattern, the MO, the eerie familiarity of the crime scenes. It was as if The C.K KILLER was leaving a trail of breadcrumbs, taunting them, challenging them to catch him.

Mike, too, was deeply affected by the truck driver's testimony. The rawness of the account, the fear in the man's voice, brought the reality of the case into sharp focus. They were dealing with a monster, a ruthless predator who preyed on the innocent.

As the call ended, Sarah and Mike exchanged a knowing glance, and herd the old truck driver say it was a red Peterbilt truck. The truck driver's account had breathed new life into the investigation, providing a tangible lead, a potential path to the killer.

Sarah, her determination renewed, turned to Mike. "Let's go," she said, her voice filled with purpose. "We need to track down that truck and the man who was driving it."

Mike nodded in agreement, his eyes reflecting the same determination that burned in Sarah's. They were on the trail of The C.K KILLER, and this time, they wouldn't let him slip through their grasp again.

Together, they delved into the details of the truck driver's account, scrutinizing every word, every description. They tracked down the partial truck's license plate number and began tracing its movements, their investigation leading them across state lines, into the heart of the country's vast network of highways.

The chase was on, a relentless pursuit through the shadows, guided by the echoes of the truck driver's voice, the haunting reminder of the C.K KILLER reign of terror. Sarah and Mike were determined to bring him to justice, to end his reign of terror, and to bring peace to the families of his victims.

CHAPTER 4: Whispers in the Night

Detective Sarah Jensen and Officer Mike Mullins went back to the scene of Tammy Williams body dump site. Looking through the area for clues of something that she feel the C.K Killer have left behind, with the help of Detective Wilbert Smith, an homicide detective for Binghamton New York Police department who was the first detective on this case. Detective Smith knew that this was not just some random act killing of Tammy Williams. Tammy Wiliams was known in the area to be a young lady who was destine to be a model one day in the New York fashion world. She was six feet four inches tall, slender built and a mother of a five month old daughter. She worked part time at the Pilot Truck Stop over the weekend schedule.

Detective Sarah Jensen and Officer Mike Mullins sifted through the underbrush, their flashlights cutting through the darkness like blades. The rustle of leaves and the distant hum of the night enveloped them as they combed the area for any shred of evidence. The cold wind whispered secrets, but the truth remained elusive.

As they meticulously worked the crime scene, Detective Wilbert Smith's seasoned eyes caught a glint in the shadows. He bent down and retrieved a small, tarnished gold locket from the ground a few feet away was a white cloth. Engraved initials hinted at a personal connection. But what he noticed on the cloth was a initial C.K... Could this be a key to unlocking the mystery?

The trio huddled, their breath visible in a slight windy breeze, as Detective Smith shared his insights. "Tammy Williams wasn't just a random target," he said. "She had a life, dreams, and someone who cared about her, like a beautiful baby girl who is all along now, and will never remember her mothers life."

Sarah, deep in thought, recalled the bits of Tammy's life they'd uncovered. She had dreams and goals of being a fashion model, she had a part-time job, a baby daughter—her existence painted a picture of aspirations, abruptly cut short by a killer who didn't care about her or anything attached to her.

As the night pressed on, the detectives unraveled threads of the victim's life, each revelation intensifying the need to stop the C.K KILLER before another life fell victim to the shadows of the elusive killer.

As they investigated, a silent dialogue unfolded between them—subtle glances and exchanged thoughts, a cohesive unit committed to solving the puzzle that sprawled before them. The slight breezy wind whispered through the trees, as if carrying the secrets of the night, secrets that held the key to apprehending the elusive killer.

"This wasn't a random act," Detective Smith asserted, his voice cutting through the quiet night. "Tammy Williams had a story—a life beyond this grim trauma."

The trio regrouped, huddled in the cool breezy night air, their collective breath visible in the darkness. Detective Smith's gaze bore into the distance, contemplative and determined. "We need to look deeper into Tammy's life, find connections, and understand why she became a target. This killer has a method, a purpose. We just need to uncover it."

The investigation intensified, the detectives sifting through the victim's past, following the threads that led them deeper into the labyrinth of motives. The Pilot Truck Stop, Tammy's coworkers, and her acquaintances became focal points as they sought to untangle the complex web surrounding her life.

As hours passed, the night grew darker, and the forest seemed to close in around them. Whispers of the wind carried echoes of the investigation, the cryptic clues, and the urgency to prevent another tragedy. Each step brought them closer to the truth, but the path ahead remained shrouded in shadows.

Back at the station, the detectives gathered their findings. Photos of Tammy, witness statements, and the enigmatic locket lay scattered across the table—a mosaic of evidence demanding scrutiny. Detective Smith, with his years of experience, guided the conversation, urging Sarah and Mike to question every lead, no matter how uncomfortable it is.

The room became a nexus of determination, a shared commitment to bringing justice to Tammy Williams and, by extension, to all potential victims of the C.K KILLER. The investigation, like a relentless river, flowed onward, fueled by the collective resolve of those sworn to protect and serve.

As dawn approached, casting a feeble light through the station windows, the detectives knew that time was both their ally and their adversary. The C.K KILLER, a phantom in the night, left behind a trail of fear and uncertainty. But within the walls of the investigation room, a flicker of hope remained—a beacon fueled by the tireless pursuit of truth.

The next phase awaited, with challenges yet unseen and a killer whose motives lingered in the shadows. Detective Sarah Jensen, Officer Mike Mullins, and Detective

Wilbert Smith stood at a steep cliff to climb, ready to face the darkness head-on, determined to unravel the enigma of the C.K KILLER.

Chapter 5: The Sinister Mile

Sarah and Mike Mullins sped along the highway, the headlights of their unmarked police car cutting through the darkness. The tension in the air was palpable, their minds consumed by the recent discovery of the white cloth bearing the initials "CK." – a chilling signature left behind by The CK KILLER.

The confirmation of their suspicions had ignited a renewed fire within them, a determination to bring the elusive killer to justice. The weight of the case pressed heavily upon their shoulders, but they were driven by the memory of the victims and the unwavering belief that they would ultimately prevail.

As they approached Rogersville, their hometown, Sarah turned to Mike, her voice laced with a mixture of urgency and determination. "Mike," she began, "I need to ask you something."

Mike, his eyes focused on the road, responded with a curt nod. "What is it, Sarah?"

Sarah took a deep breath, her heart pounding in her chest. "Do you remember Greg Abbott Jr.?" she asked hesitantly.

Mike's grip tightened on the steering wheel, his expression hardening. "Of course," he replied, his voice laced with a hint of bitterness. "How could I forget?"

Greg Abbott Jr. had been a prime suspect in The CK KILLER case, but the lack of concrete evidence had forced them to release him. The thought of him still walking free, potentially responsible for the heinous crimes, gnawed at Mike's conscience.

Sarah's eyes met Mike's in the rearview mirror. "I know it's a long shot," she admitted, "but I can't shake the feeling that Greg Abbott Jr. is somehow involved in these killings. The timing, the pattern, the meticulousness of his actions – it all fits too well."

Mike nodded thoughtfully, considering Sarah's words. "I know," he agreed, "and I hate to admit it, but you're right. There's something about him, something that just doesn't sit right with me."

A surge of determination coursed through Sarah's veins. "Then we need to look into him again," she declared, her voice filled with conviction. "We can't let this go. We owe it to the victims, to their families."

Mike nodded in agreement, his eyes reflecting the same determination that burned in Sarah's. They were determined to reopen the case against Greg Abbott Jr., to uncover the truth that had eluded them for so long.

As they pulled into Rogersville, the lights of the small town twinkled like distant stars, a stark contrast to the darkness that shrouded their mission. The chase was on, and this time, they wouldn't rest until they brought The CK KILLER to justice.

Sarah got back to her desk, exhaustion etched into the lines on her face. The harsh fluorescent lights of the police station flickered overhead as she settled into her chair. The hum of activity in the bustling office seemed to fade away, leaving only the weight of the ongoing investigation on her shoulders.

As she powered up her computer, Sarah noticed an urgent email from the Chicago PD. The subject line sent a shiver down her spine: "Critical Clue Uncovered in Double Homicide." Sarah screamed "Dammit!!, I knew it" and the whole room got quiet that you could hear a pin drop.

Opening the email, she absorbed the grim details. Two murders, both on the same street, hours apart. The victims, young women, had suffered a brutal fate—beaten and raped. The similarities to Dianas' and Tammy Williams' case were chilling, forging an ominous connection across state lines.

Sarah's mind raced as she delved into the provided information. The Chicago detectives, in the course of their interviews, stumbled upon a crucial leed: two white striped cloths bearing the unmistakable initials C.K. These letters, etched into the fabric, mirrored the dark signature of the C.K KILLER.

A sense of urgency surged through Sarah. The interwoven threads of these cases created a tapestry of terror that stretched beyond the borders of Pennsylvania and New York. The killer's sinister reach now extended to Chicago, leaving a trail of victims in his wake.

Sarah recalls the interview when she questioned Greg Abbott Jr's whereabouts. He stated that he was heading to Chicago area to visit his family for a few hours before delivering his load to Saint Joseph Kansas that was on his bill of lading she recalled.

She immediately contacted Detective Smith and Officer Mullins, briefing them on the new developments. The trio swiftly convened, strategist on how to collaborate with the Chicago PD and leverage the shared information to crack the case wide open.

The hours blurred as they coordinated efforts, sharing insights and pooling resources. The connection between the cases painted a haunting picture of a serial predator traveling the country, leaving devastation in his wake. Each victim, a tragic note in the chilling symphony orchestrated by the C.K KILLER.

As the sun dipped below the horizon, casting long shadows in the police station, a joint task force took shape. Detectives from different jurisdictions, bound by a common goal, worked tirelessly to decipher the cryptic clues left by the elusive killer. The urgency of the situation propelled them forward, a collective force determined to bring an end to the reign of terror.

The investigation unfolded on multiple fronts. Forensic experts analyzed the white striped cloths, hoping to unveil any trace of the perpetrator. The F.B.I Behavioral analysts delved into the psyche of the killer, seeking patterns and motives that could guide the pursuit. The collaboration between agencies, once distant entities, now became a unified front against a common foe... The C.K KILLER..

Sarah, with her unwavering determination, found herself at the forefront of this nationwide manhunt. Late nights blurred into early mornings as leads were pursued, connections unearthed, and the net tightened around the CK KILLER. The investigation became a race against time, a battle between the relentless pursuit of justice and the shadowy specter that sought to evade it.

In the heart of the storm, a breakthrough emerged. The forensic analysis yielded a match—a common fiber linking the cloths to a specific region. The clothes was handmade with with hemp fabric that is usually manufactured in Columbia South America. The killer's signature, once enigmatic, now became a breadcrumb trail leading the investigators to a potential lair.

The joint task force, armed with newfound momentum, closed in on the coordinates. The air crackled with anticipation as they approached the nexus of the investigation. The final confrontation loomed on the horizon, a collision between the forces of justice and the malevolent orchestrate of chaos.

Midnight Plea

The moon hung low in the night sky as Detective Sarah Jensen hurriedly made her way to Judge Joe Riley's house. Time was a relentless adversary, and the urgency of the situation pressed heavily on her shoulders. She knew that The CK KILLER, if indeed it was Greg Abbott Jr., wouldn't pause for her convenience. Lives hung in the balance, and the ticking clock echoed the urgency of her plea.

Arriving at the judge's residence, Sarah knocked on the door with a sense of determination. A few moments later, the door creaked open, revealing the slightly bewildered face of Judge Joe Riley.

"Detective Jensen, what brings you here at this hour?" Judge Riley inquired, his brow furrowed with a mix of curiosity and exhaustion.

"Honor, we need a warrant for the arrest of Greg Abbott Jr.," Sarah declared, cutting straight to the chase. "I can't wait until morning. Lives are at stake, and I believe we finally have a chance to bring The CK KILLER to justice."

Judge Riley hesitated, his tired eyes reflecting the weight of his responsibilities. "Sarah, it's late, and I'm having dinner with my family. Can't this wait until tomorrow?"

Sarah's gaze intensified, a silent plea for understanding. "Honor, this cannot wait. We don't have time to let this guy kill anyone else, and time is not on our side right now. Every minute counts."

Judge Riley sighed, caught between duty and personal commitments. "Detective Jensen, do not let this backfire on my head. I understand the gravity of the situation, but we must proceed with caution. If we act hastily and without proper cause, it could jeopardize the case and put innocent lives in danger."

Sarah nodded, acknowledging the judge's concern, but her eyes reflected the unwavering determination within her. "I won't let it backfire, Honor. I know we're close, and we can't afford to let this slip through our fingers. Please, help me get the warrant tonight."

Judge Riley, though frustrated, saw the fire in Sarah's eyes and recognized the relentless pursuit of justice. Reluctantly, he invited her inside, saying, "Fine, but we'll need solid evidence. If this turns out to be a mistake, it's on both of us."

As the clock continued its relentless march, Sarah and Judge Riley delved into the process of securing the warrant, driven by the shared conviction that they could not afford to let the night slip away. The CK KILLER shadow loomed, and the outcome of this midnight plea held the potential to either bring justice or deepen the enigma that had plagued Sarah for far too long.

With the warrant in hand, Detective Sarah Jensen wasted no time. The urgency of the situation propelled her into action. She swiftly organized a coordinated effort to bring Greg Abbott Jr. to justice before he could claim another victim. A warrant meant they could act, and the C.K KILLER shadow was finally within their grasp.

The red glow of the dashboard lights illuminated Sarah's determined face as she issued a BOLO (Be On the Look Out) alert for Abbott's truck. A 1987 red Freightliner semi-truck, a rolling menace that had eluded justice for too long. The information raced across police radios, flashing on screens in patrol cars, state trooper vehicles, and Department of Transportation (DOT) offices throughout the Midwest.

Sarah's voice crackled over the radio waves, "This is Detective Jensen. We have a confirmed warrant for the arrest of Greg Abbott Jr. I repeat, Greg Abbott Jr. is to be apprehended immediately. All units, be on the lookout for a 1987 red Freightliner semi-truck. This is a high-priority alert. Lives are at stake."

The night air hummed with anticipation as state troopers and DOT officers across the Midwest became the front line in the pursuit of justice. The information cascaded through the network, creating a virtual dragnet aimed at capturing the elusive killer who had haunted highways for far too long.

Every patrol car became a potential harbinger of justice, racing down moonlit highways in search of the distinctive red truck. The truck, a symbol of fear for so many, now became the beacon of hope for those desperate for closure.

As the midnight pursuit unfolded, Sarah monitored the unfolding operation from the command center. The dots on the map representing patrol cars and troopers flickered across the screen, converging on potential sightings and points of interest. The stakes were high, and The C.K KILLER was no longer a phantom. He was a tangible target, and the pursuit had become a race against time.

The red glow of the truck, an ominous specter on the highways, danced in the imagination of every officer involved. The night held its breath as the collective efforts of law enforcement wove a tapestry of pursuit, guided by the relentless determination of Detective Sarah Jensen. In the stillness of the midnight air, justice unfurled its wings, chasing shadows on the open road.

As the team prepared to find the truck location and Greg Abbott Jr, Sarah couldn't shake the haunting image of her friend Diana Hollis, Tammy Williams and the Chicago victims. Their faces, etched in her memory, fueled her determination to put an end to the C.K KILLER's reign of terror. The dark chapters written by the murderer were about to meet the unwavering resolve of those sworn to protect the innocent.

In the dim light of the control room, surrounded by the hum of computers and the urgency in the air, Sarah took a breath. The decisive moment had arrived. The hunt for the C.K KILLER was reaching its climax, and the echoes of justice reverberated through the shadows, promising resolution to those who had fallen victim to the nightmarish spree.

CHAPTER 6: Echoes of the Crime Scene

Officer Mullins and Sarah are heading to Chicago area to be there when Greg Abbott Jr is captured, she was looking through the files of the two young ladies killed the night before. Both of the women were prostitutes or what we call street workers.

As the city lights blurred into streaks, Sarah's hands moved over the photos and reports with a meticulous urgency. The images before her were more than crime scene snapshots; they were windows into the lives of two women whose stories had been brutally cut short.

"Santrice Edwards, street name Candy," Sarah murmured, her eyes fixed on the image of a young woman with a hint of defiance in her gaze. "She dropped out of high school, 22 years old, and a mother to a 9-year-old boy."

Candy's story unfolded in the pages before her—the struggles, the choices, and the resilient spirit that had propelled her forward despite the challenges. The weight of her responsibilities as a mother underscored the tragedy of her untimely end.

"And Anya Petrov," Sarah continued, her voice carrying a somber tone. "No last name, but everyone calls her White Russia. She was trafficked to the United States by the Russian mafia."

White Russia's photo revealed a woman whose eyes spoke of a different kind of captivity. The haunting shadows in her gaze hinted at a life marked by exploitation and a journey that had led her to the unforgiving clutches of the filthy and grimy Chicago streets and The C.K KILLER who ended her life.

Silence hung in the car as Sarah absorbed the details of their lives, both marked by circumstances beyond their control. The images formed a poignant tableau, a stark reminder that beneath the labels of "prostitutes" or "street workers" were individuals with dreams, struggles, and stories.

The city lights of Chicago loomed in the distance as Officer Mullins maintained a steady course. The pursuit of Greg Abbott Jr. was not just a quest for justice; it was a solemn duty to honor the memories of those who had fallen victim to his brutality.

In the quiet moments between the hum of the engine and the passing streetlights, Sarah couldn't help but feel a profound connection to the lives cut short. The echo of the crime scenes reverberated through her, fueling a determination that went beyond professional duty—it became a personal commitment to bring closure to the families of Diana, Tammy, Candy and White Russia.

As the squad car pressed on toward Chicago, the images of the four women lingered in Sarah's mind, becoming the silent witnesses to a pursuit that sought to untangle the web of darkness woven by The C.K KILLER.

In the quiet moments between the hum of the engine and the passing streetlights, Sarah couldn't help but feel a profound connection to the lives cut short. The echo of the crime scenes reverberated through her, fueling a determination that went beyond professional duty—it became a personal commitment to bring closure to the families of Diana, Tammy, Candy and White Russia.

CHAPTER 7: Pursuit Across State Lines

The squad car sped along the highway, its headlights cutting through the darkness, a beacon of hope a midst the looming shadows of the C.K KILLER reign of terror. Behind the wheel sat Detective Sarah Jensen, her eyes fixed on the road ahead, her mind consumed by the relentless pursuit of the elusive predator.

Beside her, Officer Mike Mullins, his face etched with determination, watched Sarah's every move. He knew the weight she carried, the burden of responsibility for the lives lost and the fear that gripped the hearts of countless others.

As the miles stretched out before them, the images of the four victims – Diana, Tammy, Candy, and White Russia – flashed through Sarah's mind. Their faces, once vibrant with life, now haunted her dreams, their silent pleas for justice echoing in her thoughts.

The realization that more lives hung in the balance intensified the urgency of their chase. The C.K KILLER, a phantom lurking in the shadows, was still out there, preying on the innocent. Sarah couldn't let another life be extinguished, another family shattered.

The hum of the engine and the passing streetlights provided a rhythmic backdrop to their silent determination. Sarah's grip tightened on the steering wheel, her knuckles turning white as her resolve hardened. She would not rest until The C.K KILLER was brought to justice, until the families of the victims could find peace.

The road ahead was long and treacherous, but Sarah was undeterred. She was fueled by the memory of the victims, their faces her guiding lights, their unspoken words her driving force. The chase was on, and she would not stop until she had brought The C.K KILLER to his final reckoning.

The FBI, in collaboration with the local police, cross-referenced Greg Abbott Jr.'s known associates and family members living in Chicago. Armed with this information, the SWAT team executed a high-stakes operation, swiftly and forcefully breaching the doors of a location tied to Abbott's family.

However, the anticipation of capturing the elusive killer turned to frustration as Abbott was nowhere to be found. Instead, the SWAT team discovered his family, caught off guard and held at gunpoint. The tension in the air was palpable as the authorities realized that The CK KILLER had once again eluded their grasp.

The family, now detained for further questioning, became a crucial piece in the puzzle. Sarah, alongside Detective Smith and Officer Mullins, spent exhaustive hours at the police station, dissecting every detail with the hope of uncovering Abbott's whereabouts.

For several hours, the investigators probed, questioned, and pushed the boundaries of the family's knowledge. Despite the mounting pressure, Abbott's family claimed he had not attended the niece's engagement party, contradicting initial suspicions. The puzzle seemed to grow more complex with each passing moment.

Then, a breakthrough emerged from the labyrinth of uncertainty. Sarah recalled a crucial detail—Abbott's truck and a scheduled delivery in St. Joseph, Kansas. It was a lead, a lifeline in the pursuit of a killer on the run.

The investigators swiftly shifted their focus to the interstate routes, checking toll booths and scouring through video footage along the path to St. Joseph. The digital web of surveillance became their guide, tracing the journey of Abbott's truck in the critical hours following the failed raid on his family's location.

As they pieced together the timeline, a pattern emerged. The toll booths and cameras painted a vivid picture of a truck hurtling toward St. Joseph, a lone vessel carving through the night. The pursuit took on a renewed vigor as the investigators chased the digital breadcrumbs left by The CK KILLER.

As the squad car sped through the darkness toward St. Joseph, Officer Mullins broke the tense silence that enveloped the vehicle. The distant glow of city lights flickering on the horizon seemed to echo the urgency of their mission.

Officer Mullins glanced at Sarah, his voice cutting through the hum of the engine, "We're about seven hours away, Detective. You think we'll find Abbott there?"

Sarah Jensen, her eyes fixed on the road ahead, sighed. The weight of the investigation bore heavily on her shoulders, but determination flashed in her gaze. "I can't shake the feeling that we're close, Mike. St. Joseph might be where it all comes together."

Mullins nodded, his grip firm on the wheel. "It's been a long road, Sarah. You've been chasing this guy for a while now. I can't imagine what you're going through."

Sarah's gaze softened, acknowledging the shared weight they both carried. "It's not just about me, Mike. It's about the families, about putting an end to this nightmare. We owe it to them."

The city lights drew nearer, casting intermittent shadows on Mullins's face. "What do you think Abbott's game plan is? He's been one step ahead so far."

Sarah leaned back in her seat, her mind racing with possibilities. "He's elusive, knows how to cover his tracks. But every move he makes leaves a mark, a clue. We just need to piece it all together."

As the squad car continued its journey, the road stretched out like an uncharted path into the unknown. Mullins's curiosity prompted him to ask, "You think he'll resist when we find him?"

Sarah's jaw tightened at the thought. "Abbott's dangerous, unpredictable. We have to be ready for anything. But we can't let him slip away again. Not this time."

The city limits of St. Joseph began to unfold before them, a landscape of possibilities and uncertainties. Officer Mullins, breaking the heaviness with a lighter tone, said, "You ever think about what you'll do once this is over? Take a break, maybe?"

Sarah offered a faint smile. "I haven't thought that far ahead. Right now, all I can focus on is bringing justice to those who deserve it."

As they entered the outskirts of St. Joseph, the city's pulse quickened around them. The chase, now reaching a crucial juncture, demanded their full attention. Officer Mullins's gaze met Sarah's, a silent understanding passing between them—the culmination of relentless pursuit, shared burdens, and the hope that closure awaited just beyond the next turn.

CHAPTER 8: No Escape from the Horizon

As the first light of dawn painted the sky with hues of warmth, Detective Sarah Jensen and Officer Mike Mullins found themselves at the helm of a formidable pursuit. A SWAT team, comprising 15 officers from various police agencies, stood poised for action. The target: Greg Abbott Jr., the alleged C.K. Killer. An air of urgency hung thick in the atmosphere, as if time itself were pushing them forward.

The spark that ignited this renewed determination came from a tip at the distribution center. It breathed life into a dwindling flame of hope, presenting a potential breakthrough in the relentless hunt for the elusive predator who had cast a long shadow of terror across the nation. The promise of a lead injected a surge of energy into the team, transforming the pursuit into a synchronized dance with a singular goal—to apprehend a menace that had eluded justice for far too long.

Sarah gripped the steering wheel with unwavering determination, her eyes fixed on the road ahead. Every passing mile brought them closer to their quarry, each moment fueled by the memory of the victims and the unwavering belief that justice would prevail.

Mike, seated beside her, shared in her determination. His eyes reflected a mix of anticipation and caution, a testament to the years of relentless pursuit that had forged their unwavering bond. They were a team, united in their purpose, their resolve as solid as the road beneath their tires.

The landscape, now bathed in the golden hues of dawn, seemed to mirror their unwavering resolve. The towering trees stood like silent sentinels, their branches reaching towards the heavens as if in silent support of the pursuit unfolding before them.

As the hours ticked by, the anticipation mounted. The prospect of apprehending The C.K KILLER, of bringing an end to his reign of terror, sent a surge of adrenaline through Sarah's veins. Yet, she remained focused, her mind sharp, her instincts on high alert.

The distribution center loomed ahead, a beacon of hope amidst the sprawling industrial landscape. Sarah guided the squad car into the parking lot, her eyes scanning the area for any sign of Greg Abbott Jr.'s truck.

A sense of triumph washed over her as she spotted the truck, its rustic red paint gleaming under the morning sun. The unloading process was underway, but the workers moved with a deliberate slowness, a testament to the cooperation they had received from the distribution center manager.

Sarah and Mike exchanged a knowing glance, their shared determination amplified by the sight of their quarry. They were ready, prepared to bring the C.K KILLER reign of terror to an end.

The distribution center manager, understanding the gravity of the situation, had facilitated the operation, ensuring a seamless collaboration. The sun cast long shadows across the scene, as if nature itself were bearing witness to the culmination of years of pursuit.

Sarah and Officer Mike Mullins huddled together, their eyes fixed on the red truck that held the potential key to unraveling the mystery of The C.K KILLER. They meticulously went over the plan to extract Greg Abbott Jr. without causing harm to anyone else. The delicate balance between justice and safety hung in the air.

The SWAT team, a well-coordinated unit representing 15 police agencies, moved with precision. Surrounding the truck, they advanced in a synchronized dance of discipline and readiness. Guns drawn, each officer held a position, forming an impenetrable perimeter around the vehicle. The morning sun cast a glow on their determined faces, highlighting the gravity of the moment.

Sarah's heartbeat echoed in her ears as she watched the operation unfold. Every step was calculated, every movement deliberate. The shadows of anticipation danced across the pavement, creating an almost surreal tableau of law enforcement poised for justice.

Inside the truck, Greg Abbott Jr. remained oblivious to the net closing around him. The unfolding scene, an intricate choreography of law and order, concealed the imminent arrest that would bring an end to his reign of terror.

As the SWAT team closed in, Sarah felt a mixture of tension and resolve. This was the moment—the culmination of sleepless nights, tireless pursuits, and unwavering dedication. The air crackled with anticipation, a silent symphony of law enforcement converging on the elusive predator.

With the truck surrounded, the extraction plan in place, and the sun casting its first light on the scene, Sarah Jensen knew that this was more than an arrest; it was the reclamation of justice. The C.K KILLER, cornered and exposed, was about to face the consequences of his malevolent journey across the highways of the nation.

As the SWAT team executed their precision movements, a subtle ripple of awareness spread through the surrounding area. Other truckers, drawn by the unusual spectacle, began to watch the unfolding drama. Their curiosity piqued, they observed the synchronized ballet of law enforcement, their eyes trained on the unfolding scene.

In the expansive parking lot of the distribution center, a silent audience emerged. Truckers, each with a rig of their own, peered out from their cabs or stood atop their trailers, keenly observing the drama that was playing out. The distinctive hum of idling engines provided a steady undercurrent, a symphony of anticipation.

Then, like wildfire, the news of the C.K KILLER capture spread among the truckers. A collective realization dawned, and cell phones emerged from pockets, capturing the momentous event. The scene became a mosaic of screens, as truckers went live on Facebook and TikTok, their social media platforms becoming impromptu broadcasts of justice in action.

In the midst of the operation, Officer Mike Mullins glanced at the growing audience. "Looks like we've got an audience," he remarked to Sarah, a wry smile playing on his lips.

Sarah nodded, her attention focused on the task at hand. The weight of the moment, amplified by the watchful eyes of those unexpected spectators, added a layer of complexity to the already tense operation. The line between justice and public spectacle blurred as the truckers documented the SWAT team's meticulous movements.

The rhythmic click of camera shutters and the soft glow of lights illuminated the movement. The live streams captured every twist and turn of the extraction, turning the distribution center into an impromptu stage for the nation to witness the end of the C.K KILLER reign of terror.

As the SWAT team closed in on the red truck, the live feeds broadcast to millions of there followers all over the country, the climax to an audience beyond the immediate scene. The comments section filled with a mix of disbelief, relief, and anticipation. The truckers, once passive observers of the highway's mysteries, became inadvertent documentations of a pivotal moment in law enforcement history.

In the end, the C.K KILLER capture became not just a triumph of justice but a shared experience etched into the collective memory of those who bore witness to the relentless pursuit that unfolded on the highways and byways of the nation.

The Confrontation

All at once, the air crackled with tension as the SWAT team executed their meticulously planned extraction. The symphony of precision turned discordant with the staccato chatter of guns and the authoritative commands of police officers cutting through the morning air.

"Freeze! Get out of the truck!"

The scene erupted into a cacophony of voices as the officers closed in on the red truck. The truckers who had been silent observers now witnessed the intense confrontation unfolding before them. The live streams continued, capturing the drama as it unfolded in real-time.

Over the chaos, the commanding voice of Officer Mike Mullins rose, amplified through the loud horn, reaching the confined space of the red truck where Greg Abbott Jr. sat unaware of the storm closing in around him.

"Greg Abbott Jr.! We have a warrant for your arrest. Get out of the truck with your hands up, if you make any settlen moves, we will kill you!"

The gravity of the situation echoed through the distribution center's parking lot. The truckers, now active participants in the unfolding events, shifted their focus from their own cabs to the scene of confrontation. The live streams captured every nuance, from the tension in the officers' voices to the seemingly innocuous red truck that had become the epicenter of a nationwide manhunt.

Inside the truck, Greg Abbott Jr., now confronted by the harsh reality of his crimes catching up with him, faced a pivotal choice. The world outside awaited his response, and the officers held their breath, fingers poised on triggers, as they awaited his surrender.

The air felt heavy with anticipation as the seconds stretched into an eternity. The red truck, once a symbol of anonymity on the vast highways, had now become a stage for the reckoning of The C.K KILLER.

As the live streams broadcast the standoff, the collective gaze of the nation fixated on the red truck at the distribution center, where justice hung in the balance. The confrontation had escalated from a clandestine pursuit to a public spectacle, a testament to the evolving nature of crime and punishment on the open road.

As the SWAT team closed in, Greg Abbott Jr.'s world unraveled before him. Shock contorted his features, and his protests echoed through the distribution center.

"Why? What did I do? I'm innocent! Please, don't kill me! I didn't do anything!"

The pleas filled the air, a desperate refrain that clashed with the surrounding chaos. The truckers, transfixed by the unexpected turn of events, continued to document the unfolding drama through their live streams, each frame capturing a moment in the climactic unraveling of the C.K KILLER escape.

In response to Abbott's protests, the officers wasted no time. Swiftly, they grabbed him by the back of his shirt and tackled him to the unforgiving ground. The loud thud reverberated through the parking lot, a symbol of the sudden descent from the perceived anonymity of the open road to the harsh reality of justice catching up.

As Abbott struggled beneath the weight of multiple officers, their actions carried a weight of their own—a culmination of years of pursuit, tireless investigations, and the relentless commitment to bring a murderer to justice.

Other officers joined the arrest, securing Abbott's feet and legs. The scene became a tableau of swift, synchronized movements, a visual representation of the long arm of the law reaching out to grasp a perpetrator who had eluded capture for far too long.

Knees pressed into Abbott's back, the physical restraint mirrored the emotional weight of the crimes he stood accused of. The officers, faces determined, executed the arrest with the precision that had become the hallmark of their pursuit.

As the live streams continued to broadcast, the nation bore witness to the arrest of The C.K KILLER. The shouts of innocence faded against the overwhelming evidence of his capture.

With Greg Abbott Jr. now in custody, the officers pulled him off the ground, his protests reduced to muffled gasps. Detective Sarah Jensen stepped forward, her eyes unwavering as she addressed the man whose reign of terror had left a trail of victims in its wake.

"We got you now," Sarah declared, her voice cutting through the lingering echoes of Abbott's pleas. "You are under arrest for the killings of Tammy Williams, Santrice Edwards, Anya Petrov, and Diana Holliss. "You have the right to remain silent. Anything you say can and will be used against you in a court of law. You have a right to an attorney. If you cannot afford an attorney, one will be appointed for you."

The weight of the accusations hung in the air, a stark reminder of the lives lost and the families forever changed by the C.K KILLER actions. The distribution center, once a bustling hub of commerce, now stood witness to the closure that justice sought to bring.

As Sarah recited the Miranda rights, the solemnity of the moment underscored the gravity of the charges. The truckers, who had become accidental spectators to the arrest, continued to document the proceedings, their live streams capturing the final chapter of a manhunt that had gripped the nation.

CHAPTER 9: The End Of The Chase

The news of Greg Abbott Jr.'s arrest spread like wildfire, igniting a frenzy of media attention. As the local news station arrived at the scene, their cameras captured the aftermath of the chaotic arrest, the warehouse still echoing with the lingering tension of the entire excitement of the C.K KILLER's end of terror.

Sarah Jensen and Officer Mike Mullins stood a midst the commotion, their faces etched with the weariness of battle and the relief of victory. They had faced The C.K KILLER and emerged victorious, bringing an end to his reign of terror.

The reporters, their voices eager and insistent, bombarded Sarah and Mike with questions, their microphones thrust forward like weapons in their quest for information. The air crackled with anticipation, the public hungry for details, desperate to understand the events that had unfolded.

Sarah, her voice steady despite the lingering adrenaline, addressed the reporters, providing a brief account of the arrest. She spoke of Greg Abbott Jr., The C.K KILLER, and the years-long pursuit that had led to his capture.

Mike, his expression grim, nodded in confirmation, his eyes scanning the crowd for any sign of disturbance. The arrest had brought a sense of closure to a dark chapter in their lives, but they knew that the scars of their experiences would remain.

As the news of Greg Abbott Jr.'s arrest reverberated across the nation, the families of the victims, those who had endured unimaginable grief, found a glimmer of hope amidst their sorrow. The C.K KILLER, the phantom who had haunted their dreams and shattered their lives, was finally behind bars.

The nation breathed a collective sigh of relief, the fear that had gripped them for so long slowly dissipating. The C.K KILLER reign of terror had ended, and a sense of justice, however belated, had been served.

The car rumbled along the highway, the landscape rolling by as Detective Sarah Jensen, Officer Mike Mullins, and Detective Wilbert Smith escorted Greg Abbott Jr. back to Rogersville, Pennsylvania. The weight of the truth and the impending trial hung in the air, each passing mile marking the journey towards justice.

In the confined space of the car, Greg Abbott Jr.'s protests persisted, a relentless drumbeat of denial that echoed through the vehicle. Every few minutes, he insisted on his innocence, his words cutting through the ambient hum of the engine.

"I didn't kill anyone," Abbott Jr. declared, his voice wavering with a mix of desperation and defiance. "I'm a married man, a father of five kids. I've never hurt or killed anyone. I'm a faithful husband."

The repetition of his innocence became a dissonant refrain, a stark contrast to the evidence that had led to his arrest. The detectives exchanged glances, acknowledging the predictable rhythm of a suspect clinging to the last vestiges of denial.

Detective Sarah Jensen, though accustomed to such proclamations, maintained a stoic composure. "Greg, the evidence tells a different story. We have witnesses, a trail that leads directly to you. The jig is up."

Officer Mike Mullins, steering the car with focused determination, interjected, "You can tell it to the judge, Mr. Abbott. The court is where you'll have your chance to plead your case!."

Detective Wilbert Smith, silent for most of the journey, observed the unfolding dynamic. "You've got a right to defend yourself in court, Mr. Abbott. That's where we'll let the evidence speak."

Yet, Mr. Abbott Jr. persisted in his protestations, each declaration a futile attempt to rewrite the narrative that had led to his arrest. The car, a microcosm of conflicting truths, continued its journey through the vast expanse of the highway.

As the miles ticked away, the echoes of denial filled the car, an audible reminder of the complexities that lay ahead. Rogersville awaited the arrival of justice, and the truth, no matter how vigorously denied, would unfold in the halls of the courtroom.

CHAPTER 10: Shadows of Doubt

The trial loomed on the horizon, a specter casting its long shadows over Rogersville. The small town, once relieved by the arrest of Greg Abbott Jr., now found itself caught in the uneasy grip of uncertainty. The whispers of doubt crept through the community, weaving a tapestry of skepticism that threatened to unravel the tightly wound threads of justice.

In the days leading up to the trial, the media descended upon Rogersville like a swarm of vultures, hungry for any morsel of information that could sensationalize the case. The once-celebrated heroes, Sarah Jensen and Officer Mike Mullins, now faced scrutiny as doubts regarding the evidence began to surface.

The defense, led by a seasoned attorney named Evelyn Chambers, seized upon the opportunity to exploit the cracks in the prosecution's narrative. Chambers, a master of manipulation in the courtroom, cast doubt on witness testimonies and questioned the validity of the forensic evidence that had seemed so damning.

As the trial commenced, the tension in the courtroom was palpable. The families of the victims, their hopes pinned on the pursuit of justice, watched anxiously as the legal proceedings unfolded. Greg Abbott Jr., maintaining his facade of innocence, faced the scrutiny of the jury and the eyes of a nation that had, just days before, exhaled in collective relief.

The prosecution presented its case with unwavering determination, unveiling a meticulously constructed timeline of the C.K KILLER's atrocities, all seemingly leading back to Abbott Jr. Witnesses took the stand, recounting harrowing experiences and pointing accusatory fingers at the man who sat stoically in the defendant's chair.

Evelyn Chambers, however, danced through the legal proceedings with a grace that left the prosecution stumbling. She skillfully planted seeds of doubt in the minds of the jury, exploiting any inconsistency in the evidence to create a narrative of uncertainty. The defense argued that the real killer was still at large, lurking in the shadows, while Abbott Jr. languished in a jail cell.

As the trial unfolded, the once-solid case against Greg Abbott Jr. began to show hairline fractures. The prosecution, burdened by the weight of public expectation, struggled to counter Chambers' persuasive tactics. The town, torn between its desire for closure and the unsettling possibility of a miscarriage of justice, held its breath.

CHAPTER 11: A Twist Unveiled

A midst the turmoil of the trial, Detective Wilbert Smith delved deeper into the case, determined to uncover any overlooked detail that could bolster the prosecution's case. Late nights were spent poring over files, re-interviewing witnesses, and examining forensic reports with meticulous scrutiny.

In a dimly lit room at the police station, Wilbert stumbled upon a lead that had gone unnoticed—a series of unexplained discrepancies in the timeline of the murders. As he pieced together the puzzle, a realization dawned: the possibility that there might be an accomplice, a shadowy figure working in tandem with the incarcerated Greg Abbott Jr.

Wilbert's heart raced as he traced the connections between the murders. There were subtle, almost imperceptible variations in the methods used and the times the crimes were committed, suggesting a different hand at work in some instances. The theory of a single perpetrator began to crumble, replaced by a more sinister possibility—a partnership steeped in darkness.

With newfound urgency, Wilbert brought his findings to Sarah Jensen and Officer Mike Mullins. The trio, now facing the very real prospect of a flawed conviction, grappled with the implications of this revelation. The walls of the police station seemed to close in as they considered the ramifications of a potential second killer still roaming free.

Sarah leaned forward, her brow furrowed in concentration. "If there is an accomplice, we need to figure out who it is and fast. The trial won't wait for us, and the defense is already picking apart our case."

Mike nodded, his expression grim. "We can't let this go public yet. It would cause a media frenzy and could jeopardize everything. We need to investigate this quietly, under the radar."

The trio hatched a plan to discreetly investigate the possibility of an accomplice without alerting the media or the defense. They decided to revisit key locations and re-examine the evidence, hoping to uncover clues that had been missed in the initial investigation.

Their first stop was the crime scene of the second victim, a quiet suburban home that had been shattered by violence. Under the cover of night, they retraced the steps of the killer, scrutinizing every detail. Sarah's sharp eyes caught a faint mark on the windowsill, a scuff that hadn't been there before. It was a small detail, but in a case like this, even the smallest detail could be significant.

Next, they visited the scene of the fourth murder, a dimly lit alleyway behind a row of shops. As they scanned the area, Wilbert noticed something odd—a faint, oily residue on the ground, leading away from the crime scene. He collected a sample, hoping that the forensic team could identify its source and link it to a potential accomplice.

Back at the station, they analyzed their findings, cross-referencing them with the existing evidence. The residue from the alleyway was identified as a specific type of industrial lubricant used in local factories. It was a tenuous link, but it was something to go on. They compiled a list of employees from the factories that used the lubricant, searching for any connection to Greg Abbott Jr.

As the trial continued, the defense relentlessly exploited the chinks in the prosecution's armor. They highlighted inconsistencies in the evidence and questioned the credibility of key witnesses. The prosecution struggled to maintain its narrative, while the trio worked tirelessly behind the scenes.

Their breakthrough came when they discovered a name on the employee list that matched one of the witnesses who had initially come forward with information about Greg. The witness, a factory worker named Jason Peters, had seemed eager to help the investigation but had provided conflicting statements. This new connection placed him under a shadow of suspicion.

Chapter 12: The Confession of the True Killer

Wilbert, Sarah, and Mike arranged to meet Jason discreetly. In a secluded corner of a local diner, they confronted him with their findings. Jason's demeanor shifted from cooperative to defensive as they laid out the evidence. Under the pressure, he began to unravel, his facade cracking to reveal the truth.

Jason confessed that he had been manipulated by a colleague, a man named Richard Bowen, who had been the real accomplice. Richard had orchestrated the murders, using Greg Abbott Jr. as a convenient scapegoat while Jason had provided false testimony to mislead the investigation.

Who is Richard Bowen and Why Did He Do It?

Richard Bowen was once a high school football player with dreams of greatness, but a pivotal failed play dashed those hopes forever. Settling into a supervisor role at a local power plant—secured with the help of his father, who owned the facility—Richard's unfulfilled ambitions simmered as he watched his peers advance beyond him. His fixation on Catherine Kennedy, the wife of Greg Abbott Jr., added a personal vendetta to his professional frustrations. Known for his cunning and ruthless ambition, Richard had a dark side that very few were aware of. Richard had an obsession with women who denied him, and Catherine Kennedy, who was in love with Greg, became the focus of his twisted desires. Richard also found a perverse sense of power in his interactions with prostitutes.

Why Did Richard Frame Greg Abbott Jr.?

Richard's decision to frame Greg was driven by a toxic combination of personal vendetta and the need to cover up his own crimes. By targeting Greg, Richard aimed to remove a personal rival and silence a major threat to his ongoing murders of the women he killed. Greg and the victims had uncovered illicit activities within the corporation—activities that included Richard's heinous acts. Exposure would not only end his career but also reveal him as a serial killer.

By forcing Jason, a mentally slow employee, to lie during the first interview with Detective Smith, Richard ensured that the investigation would be misdirected. Jason, overwhelmed by fear for his safety and under immense pressure, complied with Richard's demands, providing false testimony that implicated Greg Abbott Jr. in the crimes. Richard believed that with Greg as the scapegoat and Jason's coerced cooperation, he would be safe from suspicion.

However, the persistence and determination of Wilbert, Sarah, and Mike eventually led to the unraveling of Richard's scheme, bringing the true mastermind to justice. Armed with this new information, the trio knew they had to act quickly. They alerted Chief Ramirez and arranged for the immediate apprehension of Richard Bowen. The arrest sent shock waves through the town, and the media frenzy they had hoped to avoid became unavoidable.

In the courtroom, the atmosphere was electric as the prosecution presented the new evidence. The defense, caught off guard, scrambled to respond. The revelation of an accomplice changed the dynamics of the trial, casting doubt on Greg Abbott Jr.'s sole culpability and exposing a deeper conspiracy.

As the chapter closed, the town of Rogersville found itself at the cusp of a new storm. The unmasking of Richard Bowen revealed the true extent of the darkness that had gripped the town, challenging everything they thought they knew about justice and morality. The trial, now a battleground of unexpected twists, left the community grappling with the unsettling reality that the truth was far more complex and sinister than they had ever imagined.

To be continued........

EPILOGUE

The case of The C.K KILLER was a defining moment in Sarah Jensen's life. She had seen the darkness, the depths of human depravity, but she had also witnessed the resilience of the human spirit, the unwavering pursuit of justice.

She continued her work as a detective, her dedication unwavering. She carried the memories of the victims with her, their lives forever intertwined with her own. And she vowed to never stop fighting for the innocent, to protect them from the darkness that lurked just beyond the edge of light.

Tandricus R. Thomas is a dynamic entrepreneur and celebrated author who seamlessly blends his business expertise with his passion for storytelling.

As a writer, Tandricus has captivated audiences with his thrilling novel, *Detective Sara Jensen in the Chase of the CK Killer*, a gripping mystery that keeps readers on the edge of their seats. He also shares profound insights in his motivational and relationship-focused self-help books, inspiring readers to pursue their goals and build meaningful connections. Tandricus's diverse body of work reflects his commitment to empowering others, whether through his entrepreneurial ventures or the pages of his books.

Case Files of Detective Sarah Jensen

TANDRICUS R. THOMAS

IndyPublish
.com